Goldilicious

WRITTEN & ILLUSTRATED BY
Victoria Kann

HARPER
An Imprint of HarperCollinsPublishers

Goldilicious
Copyright © 2009 by Victoria Kann

Printed in the U.S.A.
All rights reserved. No part of this book may be used or reproduced in any manner whatsoever without written
permission except in the case of brief quotations embodied in critical articles and reviews. For information
address HarperCollins Children's Books, a division of HarperCollins Publishers, 10 East 53rd Street, New York,
NY 10022 www.harpercollinschildrens.com

Library of Congress Cataloging-in-Publication Data

Kann, Victoria.
    Goldilicious / written & illustrated by Victoria Kann. — 1st ed.
        p.   cm.
    Summary: A little girl and her brother play with her imaginary gold-horned unicorn that can float
on water, fly, and turn herself into a fairy princess.
        ISBN 978-0-06-124408-7 (trade bdg.) — ISBN 978-0-06-124409-4 (lib. bdg.)
    [1. Unicorns—Fiction.   2. Brothers and sisters—Fiction.   3. Imagination—Fiction.]   I. Title.
PZ7.K12774Go   2009   2008051968
[E]—dc22   CIP
                                                                                     AC

Typography by Stephanie Bart-Horvath
10   11   12   13   CG/WORZ   20   19   18   17   16   15   14   13   12   11

First Edition

To Team Pink, with love and gratitude

I was putting flowers on the mane of my pet unicorn.

"Pinkalicious, why are you dropping flowers on the rug?" asked Mommy.

"I'm not dropping flowers. I am getting Goldie ready for the
Unicorn Ball," I said, prancing around the room.

"What unicorn? I don't see any unicorn," said Peter.

"She's right here and she's not ANY unicorn, she is my unicorn.
Her name is Goldilicious, Goldie for short. Oh, Goldie—you
shouldn't have done that on the floor! You know better. Just
neigh when you need to go to the potty. I'm sorry, Peter, but you
are stepping right in it," I said.

"Mommy! What is Pinkalicious talking about?" whined Peter.

"Pinkalicious, it's okay to have an imaginary friend, but maybe it's time to put Goldie back in her stall or take her outside the house, where she can run free."

"Okay, Mommy. Come on, Goldie, we know where we aren't wanted," I said, galloping out the door.

I took Goldie out to perfect her pinkerrific pirouette. Goldie is
very graceful and has a wonderful sense of balance. We were thinking
of joining the Majestic Magenta Ballet, but there are only a few
extremely special and unique people who can see Goldie, namely, ME!

Goldie is also a pinkatastic roller skater, kite flyer, and high jumper. She is very fast. I can never keep up with her. "Goldieeeeeeeeeee, wait for me!"

"Goldie, where are you?"
She loves to play hide-and-seek, but she is
too quick for me.
As soon as I spot her, she is gone.

"Oh, you turned into a fairy princess and you are having a tea party. Goldilicious, this is the most delicious cake I have ever had! And where did you ever find this sweet flower nectar?" I asked.

"Pinkalicious, may I join your tea party?" Peter asked.

"Please, Peter, you are about to sit on Goldie! Be careful," I scolded.

"Here is a little cinnamon stick for your tea," said Peter.

"That is a WORM! Now you have insulted our host. You better watch out . . .

. . . because Goldie will always protect me!" I shouted.

"Not if I kidnap her and hold her prisoner in the castle tower!"

"Beware, fair sister, or
your golden pet will become
broth for my magical cauldron,"
Peter yelled from the tree house.

"Don't worry, Goldie, I will rescue you
from the Wandering Wizard," I said.

"Pinkalicous, you must gaze into this
crystal ball as I cast a spell," Peter chanted as
he threw a ball over the side of the tree house.
"Abracadabra, abracadin, wizard OUT, pirate IN!"

"Ahoy, matey, Goldilicious will never become your treasure! I will make you walk the plank!"

I suddenly realized that Goldilicious was nowhere to be seen.

"Hey, Peter, where did she go?"

"Look, she turned into a mermaid!" Peter pointed to Goldilicious.

"Oh, that is just her dress-up outfit. She's not a real mermaid. She is just pretending," I told Peter.

"Wow, not only can she float on water, she can float in the air. Goldilicious is flying!" said Peter.

"Come back!" I screamed.

"Will she come back tomorrow? I'm going to find my lasso so I can catch her in the morning when I wake up," said Peter.

"That's if you can find her," I yelled as Peter ran off.

"Goldie, where did you go? Have you
become one with the universe?"

"Pinkalicious, it's time to go to bed. Come in now," bellowed voices from the door.

"Perhaps Goldie is hiding from the mean sorcerers who have come to take me to the dungeon," I said loudly.

"Pinkalicious, we heard that."

"Oh, pardon me, I meant Sir Daddy and Lady Mommy, rulers supreme and gracious guardians of the Princess of Pink."
"NOW!"
"Okay, okay, I'm coming to bed, but I don't know where Goldie is, and she will miss me if I don't pet her good night."

"Oh, she was here waiting for me all along!" I said,
climbing into bed and closing my eyes.

"Sweet dreams. See you tomorrow," Mommy and
Daddy said, kissing us both good night.